Teddy Bear's Friend

Ljiljana Rylands

E. P. DUTTON

NEW YORK

First published in the United States in 1989 by
E. P. Dutton, a division of Penguin Books USA Inc.

Originally published in Great Britain in 1989 by
Orchard Books, 10 Golden Square, London W1R 3AF.

Printed in Singapore   First American Edition
ISBN: 0-525-44532-3   10 9 8 7 6 5 4 3 2 1

One fine day, Teddy was looking for his friend.
But he couldn't find him anywhere.

Teddy said to a bear on a stair,
"Have you seen my friend?"
"No," said the bear.
So Teddy went on.

Teddy jumped on his bike.
He whizzed past some bears with balloons.
"Have you seen my friend?" said Teddy.
"No," said the bears.
So Teddy went on.

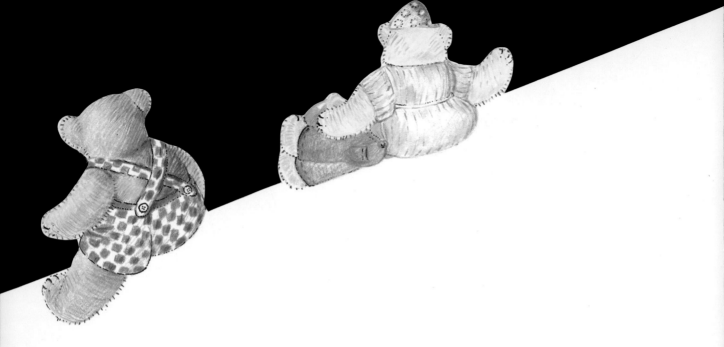

He came to some bears reading books
and a bear with a bun.
"Have you seen my friend?"
"No," said the bears.
So Teddy went on.

He came to some bears busy painting.
"Have you seen my friend?"

"No," said the bears.
So Teddy went on.

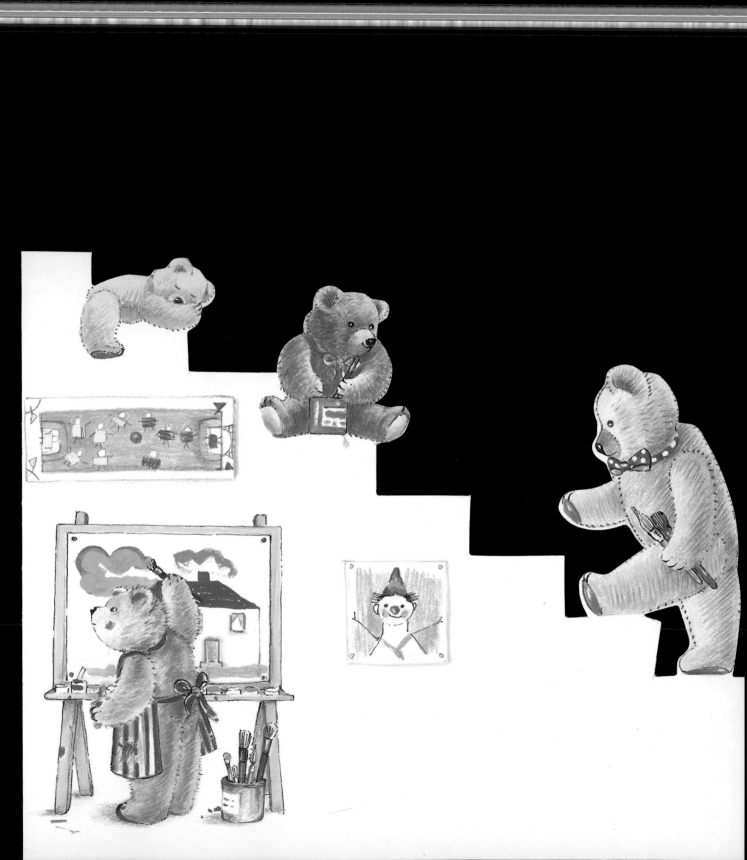

He came to some bears with their papa.
"Have you seen my friend?"
"No," said the bears.
So Teddy went on.

He came to some bears on roller skates.
"Have you seen my friend?"
"No," said the bears.
So Teddy went on . . .

and on and on.

Finally Teddy came to his friend's house.
He stood on tiptoe to look through the window.
And there was . . .

his frien
Teddy's
ran to th

his friend!
Teddy's friend
ran to the window.

"Where have you been?" said Teddy.
"Right here," said his friend,
"having tea with my family."

Then they both went out to play.